ESTHER BEAN
The Queen
OF
Self~Esteem

WRITTEN BY:
JACQUELINE NORWOOD-HALL
Illustrated By Yoko Matsuoka

TX-8-124-315
ISBN: 978-0-578-16246-1

DEDICATION:

This book is dedicated to my children Miyah, Praise, Gabriel, Biancah, Theodore, Isadore Jr. and Zyan. May you continue to use your magnetic power to affect change in your family and community for generations to come.

4

This is Esther Bean.

Esther's respectful, so kind and polite.
To see others happy brings her such great delight.

When a teacher is speaking, she pays real close attention.
She zips her lips tight, while her ears start to listen.

When someone's out sick, home from school on that day…
She calls them right up, making sure they're okay.

She says please and thank you,
when asking for more.
She picks up the lunch trash that's
left on the floor.

Not stingy or selfish, she shares
with her toys.
She divides them up equally
between the girls and the boys.

She holds the door open when
recess is done.
Making her last in line and not
number one.

All the kids like dear Esther, she is sweet to the core.
All except for mean Jester, because her family is poor.

Many days, dear sweet Esther,
when she travels to school,
Has some pain in her tummy,
because her belly is not full.

And the times during recess
when she hides behind rocks,
Is so Jester won't tease her about
the holes in her socks.

Esther would close her eyes and
make believe if only for a day,
She were queen in a castle, in a land
far away.

In this land far away, she would be
a great queen,
She would banish unkind people,
like the cruel Jester Mean!

But when Jester does spot her,
He'd summons the crowds.

Make big fun of her teeth,
Laughing long, hard and loud.

Pointing out her old shoes or her
pants with the stains.
Poking fun at her tight coat,
mocking her with disdain.

"Esther, Esther, she's no queen!
With holes in her socks and her
pants are unclean!"

Esther would try, oh she'd try, yes she'd try, how she'd try,
She would close her eyes tight, she would try not to cry.

But she would.

All by herself...

When Esther went home after
crying that day,
She told Uncle Morty, to see what
he'd have to say.

Uncle Morty told her stories that
she need to hear,
He would make her feel better and
dry all of her tears.

27

"Esther Bean, you're a queen!" Is what he would say.
"Unleash your magnetic power to brighten your day!"

"Magnetic power? What power? I don't know what you mean!"

"It is the magnetic power of a good self-esteem!"

"See yourself as the best, because you are and that's a fact!
When you see yourself clearly, only good things will attract!"

29

30

And so the next day, Jester Mean was still cruel.
He told three boys she liked them, during recess at school.

He made fun of her hair; he made fun of her coat.
He took shots at her last name, oh he'd gloat, how he'd gloat.

"Esther, Esther, Bean's no queen, with her too tight jacket
And her hair is not clean!"

Esther did try, oh she tried, yes she
tried, how she tried.
She would keep her mouth closed, as
she walked right on by.

But Jester did follow, with a crowd
right behind,
Yelling, "Look at Esther's big glasses,
she can't see because she's blind!"

Then the crowd started laughing, with
a rip and a roar.
"Esther Bean!" They started chanting.
She couldn't take it anymore.

"Listen here, you cruel mean Jester, because I've had about enough! Watching while you taunt and pester, poor little kids about their stuff!"

"Does it matter that my socks have holes, or that my jacket is too tight? Does it matter that my shoes need soles, or that my glasses don't fit right?"

"Does it matter that my pants have stains and that I don't have another pair?
Does it matter that Bean is my last name or that I have kinky hair?"

"It only matters when you make it,
poking fun of what is seen.
You can dish but you can't take it,
because you have low self-esteem!"

"When you make big fun of others,
always pointing out their flaws,
It's your flaws you try to cover."
Jester tightened up his jaws.

Jester tried, oh he tried, how he tried to
be mean,
But before he could lash out, he was
tapped by Principal Green!

"Come with me Jester Mean, listen
good and pay attention!
March yourself right to the Dean, with
this behavior, you've got detention!"

With all of the students still gathered around, Mr. Green would now have his say.
He stooped down beside them with one knee on the ground.
And said, "What happened here today?"

"What did Esther do to you, that you heckled her so loud?
No one stood up for her or the truth, you followed right along with the crowd!"

"It takes great courage and strength to be Esther, to have good self-esteem.
It doesn't matter that Jester saw her as a pauper.
 I have witnessed the grace of a queen."

Then a hush fell over everyone. No one dared to speak a word. They couldn't believe what they had done and felt ashamed of the things they had heard.

Esther had always been real nice to them they had come to realize.
This sweet girl they laughed at was truly a gem.
And with that they apologized.

Esther felt good they had all made
amends,
It was her magnetic power that
attracted new friends.

Remember, no matter what others may say,
Use your self-esteem power to brighten your day!

The End.

DISCUSSION QUESTIONS:

1. What is self-esteem?
2. What does it take to build good self-esteem?
3. What is a bully?
4. Why do bullies mistreat others?
5. Have you ever been bullied? How did that make you feel?
6. What should you do if you are the victim of a bully?
7. Have you ever bullied someone before? Why? How did that make you feel?
8. What is a bystander?
9. Have you ever witnessed someone get bullied? How did that make you feel?
10. What should you do if you see someone else getting bullied?

ABOUT THE AUTHOR:

Jacqueline Norwood-Hall is married with seven children. She currently resides with her family in Fridley, Minnesota. Esther Bean the Queen of Self-Esteem was written with the intent to promote a healthy self-image within grade school children, especially those who are economically disadvantaged. Jacqueline enjoys spending leisure time with her family, as well as writing poetry and children's books.